WAGES OF SIN

A TALE OF THE DARK DESIGN
BY NILS NISSE VISSER

WITH CONTRIBUTIONS BY
PENNY BLAKE & NIMUE BROWN &
DUKE BOX

COVER ART BY CORIN SPINKS
ILLUSTRATIONS BY YULIYA NAZARYAN

BASED ON THE SONG *WAGES OF SIN*
BY THE DARK DESIGN

SUNG BY MISHKIN FITZGERALD
ON THE DARK DESIGN ALBUM
12 TALL TALES

WAGES OF SIN
A Tale of The Dark Design & A Sussex Smugglepunk tale

Written by Nils Nisse Visser
Cover Design by Corin Spinks
Model: Lara Blair from Shimmy Armageddon & The Boxes of
Chaos Performance Troupe.

Published by CBS GREEN MAN PUBLICATIONS
Brighton, Sussex, 2020/2021
ISBN: 978-1-9162342-5-3

Based on the song 'Wages of Sin' by The Dark Design, on their
album 12 Tall Tales. Lyrics used with kind permission.

DEDICATED TO
JOHN RYAN &
RUSSELL THORNDIKE

The wages of sin, it's a bottle of gin

And memories you'd rather forget

It's growing old alone, so bitter, so cold

Add ice, lemon, and regret

From 'Wages of Sin' by The Dark Design

ROMNEY MARSH –
TUESDAY 31 OCTOBER 1871

<u>Scylla</u>

Damned memories. I reckon the musicians are to blame. I want to drown the lot of them in the vilest mud I can find in the marsh.

<u>Tess</u>

Though not as commonplace as I would have liked, it wasn't a rarity for a group of wandering musicians to show up at the Mairemaid Inn in Sinneport, offering their skills in exchange for a bite to eat, a drop to drink, a place to sleep, and a handful of coins.

Scylla was wary, but then, she trusted nobody at all. I knew well enough that a good performance could whet appetites and keep the ale flowing.

I wasn't sure about this bedraggled bunch though; they seemed a proper mishmash. The group seemed lost, out of place – perhaps not even fully aware of where they were. And if they were that out of touch, would they know what they'd be doing when they unpacked their instruments?

Three of them stepped forward.

The first had long, wild, silver-streaked black hair. He had a greying moustache and frumious beard. His garments suggested he was a North American frontiersman of sorts, fresh out of the wilderness after a spell of trapping beavers and wrestling grizzly bears.

The second was dressed as an educated gentleman, albeit in khaki tropical gear, pith helmet and all. It was a strange sight to behold on a grey, wet, and chilly English autumn day, more something I would have expected to see worn by a colonial official ambling along the dusty and sleepy main road of a provincial township baking in the midday sun.

The third was clad in old-fashioned sailing gear that wouldn't have looked out of place a century ago – but that wasn't uncommon along the south-east coast. Top hats and bowlers were prevalent along the boulevards of the fancy sea-side resorts, but elsewhere old-fashioned tricorne hats were still stubbornly worn in defiance of high society's fashion fads.

"Are ye any good?" I challenged the musicians. "Or do ye reckon I'm a soft touch?"

The sailor's eyes grew wide with indignation. He indicated the grizzly-man. "Othniel Cope is from Lye Street."

His tone suggested instant awe was a suitable response, but Sinneport was isolated. The town looked much like it did centuries ago, bypassed by most of the wonders brought about by the Age of Steam, and no longer host to a steady flow of travellers who brought us news from the outside world. I shrugged off my ignorance. Since I had never heard of the place, I decided it was safe to assume it wasn't anywhere nearby. "A fair stride from Romney Marsh."

"That may be, Ma'am," the grizzly-man spoke, his accent touched with an echo of Scotland. "But there are no finer musicians in the realm. We tickle ears, conjure smiles, command laughs, direct feet, blister toes, summon tears, melt hearts, caress souls, and warm loins."

I stared at him. He was possibly not quite right in the head. It all sounded very fine, but I had to make a business decision for which I required facts, not flights of fancies.

"Goody Hawkhurst," the prospector spoke in reasoned tones. "Your reputation as a shrewd...erm...*innkeep* has spread far beyond the fair town of Sinneport."

"Over the hills and far away," Grizzly-man supplied helpfully.

Prospector ignored him and continued, "We are all of us possessed with a healthy sense of self-preservation, Goody Hawkhurst. Thus, we make no idle boasts. We desire to depart these parts with pockets weighed down by fair begotten coin and heads firmly attached to shoulders."

I was pleased with Prospector's response. He demonstrated a good understanding of how things worked out here on this forgotten edge of England and was entirely correct in assuming my wrath was something best avoided. That kind of clarity formed a good basis to build an agreement on.

I thought I heard thunder in the distance, over the bay, and cast an eye at the cloudy sky that held the threat of rain.

"It be coarse weather, ye'd better come in," I told them. "Warm yerself by the fire in the taproom, and we'll parley[1] terms."

Scylla

Lies! Spies! There's something unsavoury about this lot. Send them on their way, or better yet, give them to me to play with…

Tess

The musicians were allocated a corner of the tap room and began to unpack and tune their instruments. I requested two sets. A short one to earn their supper. A longer one, later this evening, for bed and breakfast.

I wanted to determine if they were anywhere near as good as the wild promises made by Grizzly-man, before committing the inn to a full evening of this odd lot. If they disappointed me, they'd get their supper as promised, and would then be invited to depart with haste.

Other than that, my tap-room was filled with Mairemaid Inn 'regulars'. In these parts it wasn't odd

---

[1] Parley, or Parly meant to talk in Broad Sussex idiom.

for an inn-keep to employ a dozen or so rough men and women who were never seen to be doing anything other than eating the larder empty and drinking the cellars dry. If they were any good, their other activities remained unseen and unsung.

My lot, the Mudlarks, were good. Best in the business as far as I was concerned. Half of them would have to brave the Rozzers[2] and the chill later that night on a run to the salts of Walland Mush, to collect a crop of tea brought ashore the old-fashioned way, over sea by means of a barque out of Boulogne. The men and women I'd selected for the task would go without hesitation, but I knew they'd be disappointed to miss the music. The early set I asked for also served to let them partake in the entertainment. I looked after my crew, I always had.

There were a few irregulars present as well. If these townsfolk liked what they heard, news of musicians at the Mairemaid would spread through Sinneport like wildfire. Later that night the taproom would fill up with folk seeking to escape small-town life on a dismal autumn's eve.

I sat down by the bar with a gin in hand to observe the band when they launched into their first set.

---

[2] A none-too-complimentary name for those in uniform interfering with honest Free Trade business. Free Trader's jargon in the author's Smugglepunk world.

It was introduced by a man I hadn't noted before, wearing a black coat adorned with pins and badges, an open white shirt, a neatly trimmed extended goatee, begoggled top hat, and round – shaded – spectacles. Seemingly totally oblivious to the fact that the Mairemaid's taproom was relatively empty, he waved his arms enthusiastically and began to speak with enough volume to be heard at the sold-out matinee in the massive tent of a travelling circus.

"Ladies and Gents. Boys and Girls. Scaddles and Scoundrels – do heed my words as I, the one and only Duke Box and incomparable vox of—"

He was interrupted by a grizzled fisherman who shouted: "Pize, they got one of them at the Sea Pook Tavern yonder in Winchelsea."

Duke Box parried fluently: "Oh ho good sir! But you are mistaken. I know of the dreary den of despair to which you refer, and they don't have a Duke Box with a 'D' as is only proper, but a jukebox with a 'J'. It's a gaudy musical trinket that someone stuck gears, bells, lamps, and whistles on. No sir, I am the Duke of Box Hill, I am the original steampunk gent, I am the jester who dances on the road of bones. And so, I beg you good people, charge your cups, be it with ale, mead, or Brandywine. Come on now folks, do drink up, as playing for you, come here from hither and thither *and then*, we have none other than: The Dark Design!"

The musicians launched into their first song and I was pleased to note that they knew their instruments and handled them efficiently. The band certainly judged their audience well, choosing a popular favourite to kick things off. 'Bell Bottom Trousers' was received with cheers and had all singing along.

Singing bell bottom trousers,
Coat of Navy-blue
Let him climb the rigging
Like his daddy used to do!

Then early in the morning
The sailor he arose
Saying here's a two-pound note
My dear, for the damage I've done
If you have a daughter
Bounce her on your knee
If you have a son…

The Mairemaid Inn shook as if it had flown headlong into turbulent air when just about everyone in the taproom roared out the last line.

SEND THE BASTARD OUT TO SEA!

Scylla

A lot of fee-fol-diddle-dum and heigh-ho-nonny-no. Remember that French cloud buccaneer the Portuguese boiled alive on Playatown Plaza? To serve as an example to the rest of us? He sang prettier than this lot when that water started heating up.

Do you reckon mud boils? That's an interesting thought, surely it will. We could experiment. We *should* experiment. In the meantime, there is a particularly putrid mud pool near Jury's Gap, large enough to fit the whole band. Weigh them down with shot...

<u>Tess</u>

Continuing to display insight of the crowd they were playing to, enthusiasm waxing as if the band fed on the energy of their audience, the musicians launched into a rendition of 'Smuggler'.

The fiddle-dee-diddle part Scylla complained of was still an aspect of the music, but some of the musicians at the back of the group had produced different instruments, some quaint and odd looking. The use of strange instruments added fresh life to the old song, and they did something else I couldn't quite put a finger on, something that changed the rhythm and lent the familiar tune a catchy unpredictability.

I'd always liked this song and began to tap my feet on the floor.

> *Oh my love, you have a cosy bed,*
> *Cattle you have ten,*
> *You can live a lawful life,*
> *And live with lawful men.*
> *I must make do with nothing,*
> *While there's foreign gear so fine,*
> *Must I drink but water,*
> *When France is so full of wine?*

<u>**Scylla**</u>

More fol-die-diddle-dol-diddy. Unlike Tess, I'm paying attention. There is something strange about that band. It's something more than just the dress sense of the three odd frontmen, not to mention that peculiar impression they give of being here – but not quite here.

I try to count them and in doing so discover a source of strangeness. The musicians are impossible to count. The first time I count nine. Double-checking, I count ten. Then there are nine again, followed by eleven. Somehow, they are drifting in and out of the collective, and no matter how sharply I watch them, I can't see anyone arriving or departing from the group. Yet their numbers change.

I can't explain it. Then again, I don't need to. It's clearly unhealthy. They're warlocks of some sorts, sorcerers. Don't tell me these don't exist, I've seen things...far south of here, that much is true. But this has the same feel. These kinds of folk don't go anywhere without a reason and the world has taught us not to expect any kindness from strangers.

To Jury's Gap with them, I say. Weigh them with shot. Enough weight to drag them down into the mud, but not enough to hasten their ordeal. How they will squirm! Until the unrelenting inevitability of their impending death extinguishes the last remnant of desperate hope in their eyes. Always a touching moment. They'd be singing a different tune then, I'm sure.

> *Free Traders drink of the Frenchman's wine,*
> *And the darkest night is Owling time.*
> *Air Fleet Rozzers prowling astern,*
> *Landsharks awaiting beyond our bow.*

<u>Tess</u>

I couldn't resist, no-one in the taproom could, joining in with the last two lines of the chorus.

> *It's a Free Trader's life for me,*
> *Riding the clouds, like an outlaw free.*

The lines revealed a division within the ranks of my Mudlarks.

Most, the locals, emphasised the first line.

Four – five if I included myself –, put heart and soul into the second line. We sang "riding the clouds like an outlaw free" with that fierce power nostalgia can have, then glanced each other's way, exchanging knowing, barely discernible smiles.

These four I had known the longest. They had crewed for me in the south, on my airship, a converted sky-schooner called *The Parseval*. None of them required work when we had returned to Blighty, the hold filled with the accumulated treasure of twelve year's plunder. They could have retired but had chosen to stay with me and join my new profession. They were in the business for the sheer joy of it, and loyal to a fault.

Not among this tight core, in the ranks of the native Free Traders instead, was my daughter Nellie. All of nineteen years old and filled with that boundless optimism young folk have when they believe the world to be at their feet, the future promising opportunity, rather than pain, heartache, and worry.

When at last the sun comes up,
Run's crop safely stored,
Like sinless saints to church we go,
God's mercy to afford.

I looked at Nellie's cheerful face, framed by long red hair like mine.

I felt pride because of who she'd become. Intelligent, independent, compassionate, strong, and blessed with a healthy sense of humour.

I also beheld her with some sadness, because it was indeed the Free Trader's life

for Nellie as she had just joyously sung out.

It had been my desire that she learn a useful trade. I had often told her that most unhappy women I knew were dependent on men and caught in that dependency squirming and wriggling like a eels in a trap. The lesson was to have a trade and income, it allowed me, and later upon my passing Nellie, to dictate terms. Nellie had taken to inn-keeping and Free Trading like a gull to the sky, but sometimes I felt that I restricted her options. The arrangement kept Nellie from a life of continuous risk which I wanted her spared from, but which I myself missed with every fibre of my being.

> *It's the finest French for communion wine,*
> *The parson drinks it too,*
> *With a sly wink prays, 'Lord.'*

Another thundering, inn-shaking finish.

FORGIVE THESE MEN AND WOMEN, FOR THEY KNOW NOT WHAT THEY DO!

<u>Scylla</u>

Listen to them roar. In celebration of their own exploits which they no doubt consider derring-do heroism. Bah, humbug. Furtive scurrying about in the dark like hungry bilge rats in an empty hold. Running away from danger all the while, instead of facing it head on and letting gun and blade decide the outcome.

Now the sorcerers have launched into a song about writers, raising a glass to toast them even.

I toasted a writer once. It hadn't been my intention, we tended to leave passengers of seized airships unharmed. Unless they put up resistance. This bespectacled fellow, was holding on to his leather briefcase with both arms, shouting that I couldn't have it. It's hardly a clever thing to say to a pirate, is it? I made a grab for it. The idiot slashed out wildly with a knife, so I ran him through with my sword. Even as he was dying, on the ground and choking on his blood, the writer was staring desperately at his briefcase when I opened it, raising a trembling hand as if to reclaim it.

I never understood why. There was nothing of any value in there, just thousands of sheets of paper, all covered with meticulous scribbles. We consigned them to the heads on board *The Parseval*. I swear we wiped our arses with that stuff for nigh on a month, there was so much of it.

Remember *The Parseval?* You were afraid of nothing. Intercept, grapple, board, and damn the consequences. The infamous 'El Escorpion', feared along the length of the South Atlantic and Pacific coasts of Latin America, Scourge of the Caribbean. Why, the mere sight of *The Parseval* swooping down from the clouds and hoisting her colours – the white winged skull on a black field – was enough to subdue most prey into instant submission, lowering their flags, cutting their engines, and waiting passively to be boarded and parted from cargo and treasure.

Why? What on earth drove you to give up the carefree life? Riding the clouds like an outlaw free?

Tess

I continued looking at Nellie, a prime reason for retiring from my earlier career. Scylla mostly remembered the glamorous parts of it. The sheer triumph of outsmarting, outflying, and outfighting a foe. The joy of landing on a deserted stretch of tropical beach, *The Parseval's* hold filled choc-a-bloc with the contents of the larders and bars of a luxury long-haul aeroliner – good for a fortnight's or more wild feasting on warm nights beneath the bright stars of the southern hemisphere.

Scylla didn't remember the hungry, lean days. The nightmares after a crew did resist, forcing us to hack and hew our way through them to get at the loot. Proud men and women pissing and shitting themselves in terror, screaming or whimpering for their mothers at the end. The ever-present danger of betrayal when you're living with a price on your head, aware that it's all borrowed time.

I know my history. Our names echo down the centuries. Glossed over to make the anomaly of our existence something to be marvelled at. Transformed to change our harrowing motivations into a noble calling of sorts. Cleansed of our foulest deeds, or not, depending on whomsoever tells the tale.

Those who call us Queens of the Sea, or Queens of the Sky, often neglect to add that our average reigns were short, the years counted on one hand, sometimes two. Most often it's an inglorious end. There's nothing majestic about dancing the gallows jig, with a hemp necklace around your neck and the contents of bladder and bowels running down your kicking legs. Nor is there much grace dying in the corner of a shanty reeking with the stench of gangrene, screaming at the pain to go away, begging a crewmate to employ gun or blade to provide a merciful end.

I'd already beaten the odds when I gave birth to Nellie and had accumulated a tidy fortune in the process. Earlier on in my career I would have scoffed at the notion of quitting while ahead, but the arrival of a child had changed my priorities. Before, I had cared not whether I lived or died, which lent me reckless courage that is becoming in a Queen of the Sky. Afterwards, I wanted to live. Not so much for my sake as for my child's.

Fate had decreed that I myself started life in an orphanage, the lowest of the low, almost certainly destined for the short and violent life of a street girl. I'd escaped that prospect when I was thirteen, by stowing away on a cargo-zep, unaware of the destination of the airship and caring not, as long as it took me out of England.

I'd ended up in Portuguese America, the colony of Parolando, where I'd found gainful employment in the galley of a Dutch privateer on an air-flute called *De Zuidvloed*. It had been a modest start, but I'd made the best of it, and had never looked back until Nellie was born.

I didn't want my daughter to grow up an orphan. Nellie's father had died before she was born. He had been a handsome, if somewhat dim fellow with a West Country drawl, who had got himself captured by Spanish bounty-hunters. They had tortured him. To his credit, he had died beneath their knives without uttering so much as a whisper regarding my whereabouts. To the bounty-hunters he had been a means to come one step closer to earning the significant bounty on my head. To me, he had been a pleasant companion, who had surprised me by his willingness to die to protect his unborn daughter; a sacrifice I reckoned I should honour by ensuring the baby had at least one living parent left to guide her to adulthood in a hostile world.

We'd flown *The Parseval* back to Blighty, where I had paid off my crew. Every share had been enough for a comfortable retirement. As skipper, my share had been larger still. I could have lived out the rest of my life in idleness, but that kind of life would have sent me crawling up the walls screaming. Instead, with Nellie in my arms and in the company of the four crew who had refused to part ways from me, I had gone back home, to Sinneport at the eastern tip of Sussex. None remembered me, and why should they? I had been a scrawny urchin when I had fled. I returned a mature woman, with a daughter and a fortune.

I bought the Mairemaid Inn and busied myself running the inn and directing the Free Trading activities of my Mudlarks. There was some risk involved, but astonishingly low compared to the uncertainty of life as an airship pirate.

Scylla

Damn, but the bastards are seductive in their play. I cannot help but tap my feet on the floor and rap my fingers on the bar top as they launch into a reel that happens to be Nellie's favourite.

> *Oh come list a while, and you shall hear,*
> *By the rolling sea lived a maiden fair.*
> *Her mother learn'd her the Free Trade,*
> *Skirring the night sky, of none afraid.*

Tables and benches are moved to the side of the room, regulars and irregulars mix on the improvised dance floor. It's more dee-diddle-pee-piddle to be sure, not how we danced down south, but it's impossible not to be impressed by the frenetic energy that fills the taproom.

My eyes are fixed on Nellie. No song could be more apt for her and the young woman seems to know it. There's fierce joy on her face as she twirls and swirls across the improvised dance floor, eyes fixed on the broad-shouldered and handsome young man she's dancing with; Sam, one of the sons of the Old Bell's innkeep.

When did Nellie start to take an interest in these things? I often accuse Tess of being too sentimental, but now find myself surprised that the little girl I've seen grow up here at the Mairemaid has outgrown my perceptions. Watching Nellie dance with Sam leaves me in little doubt that Nellie has grown up. The way those two are looking at each other, are thrilled by the other's brief touch in dance, and the energy that radiates between them as tangible as sparks exploding from a smith's hammer striking the anvil – all of it leaves me in little doubt as to what those two will likely be up to after Nellie returns from the salts with the crop of tea.

I grin.

Good girl.

With her pistols load'd she went aboard.
By her side hung a glittering sword.
In her belt two daggers; well-armed for war
Was this fierce maiden who never fear'd a scar.

Tess

I was pleased to see Nellie happy but it was a poignant moment too. Truly Nellie was ready to start a life of her own. We had much in common, and over the last few years had become accomplices and business partners, as well as mother and daughter. None of that would fade, yet I felt like I was losing something precious.

There was a brief sense of failure too, as a mother. Possibly this was one of those times when some wise motherly advice was to be imparted, but what could I possibly say to Nellie?

Scylla

Easy. Tell her men have their uses, but it's best not to get too attached to them. They are foolish creatures. Given a hint of possible glory, they'll rush off to war and get themselves killed. Perceiving a slight to their honour, they will insist on drunkenly staggering out of whatever tavern they're in to have their face beaten to pulp outside. Granted the merest glimpse of breast or buttock, and they'll forget yours quicker than it takes for their unfastened breeches to fall to the ground.

<u>**Tess**</u>

Could I argue with Scylla's cynicism? Were the lessons I'd learned apt for my daughter? I sighed. If Nellie wanted a bit of fun with Sam, that was her right and it was what young folk do. But what if she was to lose her heart to him? Who was I to argue? There were some who grew happily old together, though outnumbered I reckoned by those who grew old together with weary resignation. Then there were all too many whose hearts were crushed, splintered, rendered, or otherwise smashed into smithereens. Was there a worse pain to bear? Was it not better to lose a hand to sabre's slash, or a leg to a cannonball?

My eyes caught those of Pug, one of my loyal Parsevals. Grinning, as if he knew what I was thinking, he raised the stump of his left arm, which now ended in a glinting, steel hook. That had been that French frégate-de-l'air which reckoned with military arrogance that *The Parseval* was easy prey. They had been caught by surprise when I turned about and drove our outgunned sky-schooner straight at them at full speed to board them. The French had put up a stiff resistance, leaving Pug with his 'scratch', as he called his artificial appendage.

I grinned back at Pug. At least a broken heart could be pieced together again, in a fashion. And then fortified to protect it from further harm. That had been my way. I'd formed temporary alliances, all our energy spent in a few magical weeks, feasting around a fire on a starlit beach, sneaking off to frolick in the surf, and then give in to feverish passion on the warm sand. It would always be over by the time *The Parseval* ascended the sky once more, letting me focus on the task at hand without distraction. Free.

Nellie's father had lasted longer than most, simply because I was with his child. There was one exception, the reason I'd encased my heart with a barrier of steel and rigidly regulated my passions in the first place.

I pushed the thought of him, the image of his face, away. Some memories are best forgotten.

The musicians finished 'Smuggler's Daughter' and had come to the end of their first set. The audience cheered and hooted appreciation. Grizzly-man approached me, a satisfied grin on his face.

"Well, Goody Hawkhurst?" He inquired.

"Ye've earned a hearty meal," I replied. "And twould please me to hear more tonight. One of my folk will show ye yer sleeping quarters, and arrange food."

He shrugged as if that wasn't of importance. "I meant the music, Goody Hawkhurst. What did you think of our music?"

I shrugged in return. "Like I said, ye've earned a bettermost meal and a comfortable bed."

Out of the corner of my eye I caught Nellie saying her goodbye to her young man, before departing the taproom with half-a-dozen Mudlarks in tow. They'd be heading down to the cellars to prepare.

Grizzly-man looked disappointed. "You speak of our art like a commodity."

"Ye've offered it to me as such," I countered, but then relented. "But if it pleases ye, ye're good enough to play at an inn where the Bard himself stayed and performed."

"I'm aware of it and honoured," Grizzly-man replied, before confusing me with utter nonsense. "I recall that performance, it wasn't half bad, considering Will had a bit of a cold and a drop more to drink than he ought to have. But our set just now...?"

"My heart only beat faster as a natural response to any well-timed riff," I told him. "There were naun shedding of tears, nor melting of hearts."

He bowed his head a little, seeming to perceive I'd already been as generous as I was going to be in my praise. "The lack of hot tears and cracked hearts, Ma'am, was out of consideration of your exalted self, a matter of courtesy, I assure you."

I laughed. "Courtesy be damned, troubadour. Do yer best I say. I tell ye what, if ye manage to move me as such in yer second set, I'll pay ye double the coin agreed upon."

"As you wish." The sparkle in his eyes told me that he had accepted the challenge. I could have warned him that scaling the cliffs at Beachy Head on a stormy night would have been an easier task than laying siege to my soul, but reasoned it was far better to have him and his musicians give it their all later.

Scylla

I make my way to the cellars, the oldest part of the inn. It's a labyrinth of passageways and ancient-barrel-vaulted chambers, including a central chamber we use to plan and debrief sea, sky, and land runs. Nellie and the half-dozen Mudlarks have just finished preparing for their run out into Walland Mush.

It's customary for Free Traders to wear a disguise of sorts when out and about. Usually this disguise isn't much more than a large scarf that can be wrapped around the face, or even just a small jute sack with holes cut out for eyes and mouth. In a similar vein Free Traders use a code name, rather than their own during an operation.

The Mudlarks take it a step further, following the example set a century before by that parson from Dymchurch. The churchman had turned into a Free Trader chief at night, riding around Romney Marsh with his men in elaborate disguises that lent supernatural terror to their appearance.

I reckon the parson had understood a thing or two about the human mind and knew a disguise serves more purpose than just hiding an identity – it can also allow the wearer to assume a different character, one who is perhaps braver and more audacious than they'd normally be. Added to that was the natural tendency of folk to be frit of the dark and be prone to all sorts of superstitions. The marsh folk spoke of the Dymchurch gang as hellish demons. It's not a bad reputation to have when your aim is to go about your business undisturbed.

Nellie – Neeva now to use her Free Trader code name – and the others have donned long dark cloaks. They've daubed their faces with white paint, with black circles around their eyes and black lines to denote nostril slits and teeth, to create a skull-like impression. Most are also wearing headgear that makes it look like as if they have tusks, horns, or antlers.

Even though I know fully well these are but disguises, and in fact it was I who had devised them, I still feel a chill steal through my bones when I enter the chamber and see all the animated, grinning skulls in the flickering candlelight.

I talk them through the mission. It's as routine as they come, and old-fashioned because the goods are being delivered by sea, rather than through the air as has become custom. Had that been the case, I would have donned my Mairemaid of Sinneport disguise and flown out with the Mudlarks on board one of our cloud-ketches, if only just to feel a feeble echo of past adventures on *The Parseval.*

As it is, the mission is ideal for Nel…Neeva to lead, though I remind them of the dangers of complacency. Sinneport's police constables will be at the Mairemaid tonight, in a drunken stupor, Tess will see to that. But there are other Rozzers to be mindful of out in the marsh. Not particularly brave ones, but they do carry loaded guns and are ill-trained in the use of them. It wouldn't be the first time a fire fight ensued simply because a Rozzer panicked at the sight of a disguised Mudlark emerging from mist or darkness.

Wishing Neeva and the Mudlarks good luck, I bid them be on their way, and they make their way into one of the secret tunnels.

I sent instructions to the kitchens that there'd be extra mouths to feed, about a dozen of them, though I wasn't entirely sure exactly how many musicians travelled in the band.

I ordered extra casks of cider and ale to be brought up from the cellars, anticipating a busier than usual evening. The remaining Mudlarks went down there as well, to mix taxed gin and Brandywine in equal measures with a recent night-time crop of Dutch Gineva and Madeira wine. The taste would be much improved as I only purchased the best for illicit import. The price would plummet because the good stuff, free of excise duties, was by far cheaper to obtain. The Mairemaid's reputation of good booze for low cost kept the inn running at a healthy profit.

I sent an errand boy to invite the town's police constables, armed with the promise of free drinks for our gallant law-enforcers. I also had a few kegs of the 'special stuff' brought up, the only partially diluted and therefore highly potent spirits I liked to serve gentlemen in uniform, in honour of their bravery in keeping Romney Marsh safe from undesirables.

All of that done, I joined the remaining Mudlarks for our evening meal and tried to relax, though that was never easy when Nellie was out on a run.

I reminded myself that she was capable and competent. Moreover, my Parsevals Pug and McFeck were by her side and Nellie was clever enough to rely on their experience and advice. Both men had known Nellie for all her nineteen years, were filled with paternal adoration of my daughter, and would die protecting her if that was needed.

Scylla

The band of travelling sorcerers, rather than finding themselves choking and gagging on vile mud as is still my advice, are given a generous meal and ample time to rest from their travels and first set.

They look refreshed, as, one by one, they start to reappear in the tap room, which is gradually filling with irregulars from town, in a mood of happy anticipation.

We are called away, alerted by those posted on the bell tower of St Mary's. Something is wrong out in the marsh. The church isn't far away, and we are used to climbing the narrow, almost tunnel-like lower stone stairs of the tower, and then the lofty and apparently ever more rickety wood ones that take us all the way to the rafters of the steeple. The view afforded by the parapet walkway is breath-taking by day, and even in the night's darkness there is a sense of great space all around.

The lookouts point, needlessly so. Gazing south-east, out over Walland Mush, there'd normally be a few clusters of lights denoting marsh villages, hamlets, and farms. It's different tonight. I retrieve my spy glass and train it on the salts between Jury's Gap and the village of Lydd. From what I can make out, four airships are flying low over the salts, each one equipped with multiple search lights, the beams of which are sweeping to and fro. From a distance, it looks as elegant as a stylised dance of sorts, but for anyone down on the ground, hunted by those beams, it must be terrifying. Worse, every now and then I can see prolonged bursts of fire from the bows of the airships. I can't hear them, but my memory provides the deathly rattle of Gatling guns.

Nellie and her Mudlarks are out there. The crop of tea was due to be collected right where those airships are prowling the salts. It's strange, for neither the Coastguard nor the Royal Aero Force normally operate in this manner, we aren't prepared for this.

I clench my jaws. Whatever is happening out there, will be over by the time we'd get there were we to rush out of Sinneport now. We can only wait, and hope that Nellie, Pug, McFeck, and the rest are keeping their heads low.

Even as I watch, the airships disengage and depart. Are they giving up their search? Or have they found and eliminated what they were looking for?

Tess will be taking this hard, no doubt. I'm made of sterner stuff. No matter how safe we want Nellie to be, Free Trading does entail risks, and our lass was bound to face a baptism of fire sooner or later.

We return to the Mairemaid, in time for the closing chorus of the shanty 'Blow the Man Down', the entire taproom singing along with gusto.

Oh, blow the man down, bullies, blow the man down
To me way aye blow the man down
Oh, blow the man down, bullies, blow him away,
Give me some time to blow the man down!

<u>Tess</u>

A woman stepped forward from the obscure group behind the band's three frontmen. I hadn't spotted her before, which was odd because of her distinct appearance. She wore a long, hooded cape, coloured a rich dark green with curling ivy stems and leaves embroidered on it in lighter shades of green. Pushing the hood back, the woman revealed a Wodewose half-mask, akin to the Green Man face, but consisting entirely of different types of leaves in their autumnal red, orange, brown, and yellow colours.

She commanded instant respect, you could have heard a sliver of Spanish silver fall on the taproom's pavestones. Folk around here go to church, but they haven't forgotten their far older roots. Most communities around here still know how to find their way to the Wise Folk, and when one of the Wise Folk desires to speak, folk listen.

She began to speak in a soft voice. "While there are green leaves on the trees, something of summer remains. When the last leaves have gone, winter has come. All Hallow's Eve falls on the tipping point between the two. The threshold between seasons, the threshold between life and death. Tonight, we remember our dead."

She began to sing, accompanied only by the beat of a hand-held drum.

> *Set a place at the table*
> *With food and drink aplenty*
> *An extra cup, an extra plate*
> *For the dead but not forgotten.*

I fought back a rising panic caused by the persistent notion that Nellie was in trouble out in the mush, and might even now be in that other world, even as the veils between the land of the living and the otherworld were lifting.

Not all that many hours ago, I had been content as content could be. Proud of my independence, proud of my achievements. No longer the mistress of two oceans, that much was true, but not unhappy to weave a web of trade, both legal and illicit, across Romney Marsh.

None of that mattered if I lost Nellie. I'd be left with nothing at all. My daughter who I had so admired on the improvised dance floor not long ago, the passion of her dance with Sam another trigger: Memories of long, hot nights a lifetime ago.

The dead, or our memories of them? Memories were a strange thing. I was at times surprised by the sheer power memories could bring about – transforming my experience of reality even; reducing the *here and now* to an insubstantial, dreamlike state and lending the *there and then* a vivid and imperative validity.

Sometimes, on an errand in town, braving cold wind and persistent rain, the merest hint of a particular smell would transport me thousands of miles and a lifetime away. Once more I'd feel baked by a tropical sun at the hustle and bustle of a market resplendent with hundreds of sights, sounds, smells…so real I would momentarily forget the misery of English weather, the responsibilities that weighed me down, the worries that kept me awake at night. Once more carefree and unconcerned about consequence, living from day to day, port to port, prey to prey.

Sounds too, could be a powerful trigger of memories. A door slammed too loud in my vicinity, and I'd be instantly alert, alive to the tiniest detail of my surroundings, feeling naked and vulnerable without the familiar weight of sword and pistols ready to snatch from my baldric. Add to that the ambiance that could be evoked by music and…

Scylla

…Some memories are best forgotten, tucked away in a dark nook of the mind behind lock and key. When they do emerge, they can do so with the unstoppable power of the fiery and sulphurous eruption of a Chilean volcano, not merely content to be present in awareness, but eager to claim their victim whole…

Tess

…and it was hardly a matter of dark design that my mind desired to dwell in times past, upon those now gone from us…

I see the smoke that circled him
I hear his footsteps, I speak his name
Hail to you upon this night
For a time you are returned.

Was it a good sign that it wasn't Nellie who appeared through the misty shrouds of memory and lives past? Instead, it was *him*. I spoke his name…

Scylla

…You speak his name. I speak his name. We speak his name, our voice one and the same…

Tess

    "Hawkeye."

I will return to you so long as seasons keep on turning.
All Hallow's Eve will call me…
…and I will rise again.

Scylla

They had held back in their first set, those damned sorcerers, now revealing – and unleashing – a powerful conviction in song and music, using those strange instruments and non-native rhythms to cast a spell upon their hapless audience. The Samhain song was followed by a Sussex lament, a favourite, yet the way of delivery made it sound like a whole new song, the impact an emotional experience anew. Their spell cast, Tess succumbed to it all too quick. I tried to wrestle control from her, but that she wouldn't allow.

<u>Tess</u>

His real name was John Kittyhawk, but he had been known as Cap'n Hawkeye.

How young we'd been, he and I. How naively convinced our love would last forever.

We had met along the shores of Rio de La Playa. I'd moved up since mustering on the Dutch air-flute, already in command of *The Parseval,* carving a bloody name for myself and my crew.

Hawkeye was a privateer, in command of the sloop *Firebrass,* not quite in the service of the King and supremely confident on his quarterdeck. I taught him to skirr the skies and was astonished by his natural aptitude for flying. Hawkeye was one of a rare breed: A Wind Reader, able to perceive movements in the sky which most cannot.

He taught me how to dance. Not the European dances in the clubs of Playatown or Decosta, where I could not venture, nor would have wanted to. Instead he took me to secret inland locations, where natives and slaves met for social occasions of their own – borrowing European traditions to add to the fusion of their own native styles. A whole new music, a whole new type of dancing. No rigid protocols, no fixed sequences. Instead, we stepped to the music and the rest was improvisation in open or closed embrace, dancing chest-to-chest, thigh-to-thigh, hip-to-hip. It was called the tangomão or tambo, frowned upon by most Europeans, but Hawkeye and I lived for those nights of non-stop dancing and we were made welcome.

We taught each other other things too, in the privacy of our cabins aboard *The Parseval* or *Firebrass*, or on lonely stretches of beach, lost and delirious in each other's arms, wanting more of the other, needing more of the other. Everything felt  right, everything felt in place, everything felt whole.

During the brief spells that our immediate desires were sated, we schemed and plotted. With our combined skills and both aerial and naval means at our disposal, we were nigh unstoppable.

We jokingly called these our Hawkish ventures, playing on our names: Kittyhawk, Hawkeye, and Hawkhurst. Drunk on love, our souls as one, we would have laughed, Hawkeye and I, had anyone told us it would all end in bitter tears.

Then she stretched forth her arms and made a great leap
From the rocks that were high to the water so deep
Saying the shells of the oysters shall make me a bed
And the shrimps in the ocean wriggle over my head.

Hawkeye and I had been planning the ultimate caper, one that would see us so rich we'd never have to work again. A Spanish ship loaded with gold. We spent hours poring over sea-charts, stolen timetables, and other titbits of information we'd gotten our hands on. Sitting naked on his bunk or mine, skins still moist and glowing after lovemaking, sipping dark rum, plotting, and scheming – dreaming of a quiet life together, even though both of us were far too restless for a quiet life. Not back then, at any rate, and I still struggle to make it work in a way that leaves my mind untouched.

We were caught by surprise when the announcement came that London and Madrid had cobbled together a peace treaty, ending all hostilities forthwith. I couldn't have cared less, but Hawkeye did.

"I'm a privateer, not a pirate," he told me. "I'll fight the King's enemies, none other."

Being a pirate, that did not sit well with me. Nor his assumption that I would follow his lead, giving up the life I'd carved out for myself at great risk. My freedom.

We disagreed. We argued. We pleaded. We shouted. We begged. We cursed. We wept. We went our separate ways.

The Spanish ship sailed across the Atlantic without incident. Our plan had required a cunning sea captain and the *Firebrass*. Impetuous as I was, I wasn't willing to risk *The Parseval* and crew in a hare-brained and hasty improvisation. Nor was I willing to forgive Hawkeye for abandoning our original plan. Abandoning what we had together.

Now every night at eight bells they appear
When the moon is shining and the waters are clear
Two constant lovers with all their young charms
Rollin' over and over - locked in love's arms.

SCYLLA

It was a brilliant and fool proof plan. More than that, it was our brainchild; it was a symbol of our union, which he rejected out of sheer stupidity.

He was an idiot. You, we, I…should have never trusted him again. But you did, didn't you? You insisted, even though I told you not to.

Crying: Oh my love's gone, the youth I adore
He's gone and I never shall see him no more.

TESS

I wanted the memories to stop – I knew where they were headed and dreaded having to relive the pain.

Stop they did, just as my heartbeat did, albeit briefly, when one of the Mudlarks I'd posted outside to keep watch came into the taproom and made straight for me.

News.

The band launched into a song about a Red Queen. The Mudlark had the sense to walk calmly. Rushing might draw undue attention to herself. Not that the local constabulary, all present, would notice, as they were practically comatose after generous rounds of the special stuff, but it always pays to be careful, if only to remain in the habit of doing so.

I kept my face neutral, to hide enormous relief upon hearing Nellie was alive and well.

"Pug follows with ponies and crop," the woman said in a low voice. "Neeva and McFeck rode ahead with the children, they be taking them to the Blue Room."

"Children? What children?"

The woman shrugged. "A boy and a girl. Chopback and Fishgut. That be all I ken."

Like the Mudlarks were from Sinneport, the Chopbacks hailed from Hastings and the Fishguts from Rottingdean.

Rottingdean.

Hawkeye was from Rottingdean. It might mean nothing, but on this night of all nights? After just having been exposed to the raw memory of him?

I left the taproom and made my way upstairs to the Blue Room. McFeck stood by the closed door. There was a pile of torn and stained garments by his feet.

"Was it bad out there?" I asked, looking at the garments.

"Nae fur us," McFeck answered. "But the bairns hae been tae hell an back. Brave, wee, scrawny things they are."

He opened the door and I stepped through.

There were two single beds in the room, tucked into corners and opposing each other. Each bed was occupied by a child, both unclothed. One of the inn's maids sat beside the boy, tending a cut across his chest. Nellie sat by the girl, who lay on her tummy, face towards the wall in the far corner. Nellie was cleaning a nasty scrape across her shoulder.

I judged the children to be ten or eleven years old. They were both covered with bruises and cuts, and both unresponsive to the treatment of their injuries.

"They're fast asleep," Nellie told me. "Goody Tumtops said they were all jawled out, flue, and beazled."[3]

"Goody Tumtops is usually right," I replied. "What happened? Are ye alright? I saw the airships over the mush, from St Mary's. Searchlights and Gatling guns."

"We'd just finished hauling the crop to the Tumtops farm when four Rozzer sky-sharks appeared. The Rozzers weren't after us, they were looking for

---

[3] Respectively: excessively fatigued, poorly, completely tired out. Broad Sussex idiom.

these two. The chavvies came stumbling out of the wetlands, all cut about and tore, shivering and soaking wet. They're both prentices." Nellie nodded at the boy. "Pip's a Chopback. Liss here a Fishgut. Their sky-skiffs were ambushed over the Channel, then pursued and brought down over the salts. The chavvies are the only survivors, they saw the rest of the crews butchered in front of them."

"Not the usual Rozzer method."

"Liss said she bain't never seen em afore, she's convinced they weren't Coastguard or Royal Aero Fleet."

"Ye used to parley my ears off, when ye were…eleven?"

"She's twelve."

"Zackly, and it didn't always make sense, to be honest."

"One of the skiffs had a Wind Reader on board," Nellie said. "It'd be a poor prentice who did not heed the words of a Wind Reader. The chavvies talk like Free Traders. Liss can read the Owler's Script, I tested her. In fact, somewhen she parlays like a regular little Owling chief, and I reckon she's as stubborn as a chief, surely."

She gave me a pointed look and I grinned feebly in response. "I bain't stubborn."

Nellie rolled her eyes. "The girl be a proper little wildcat. She was about to tackle McFeck and his great big Scottish sword with her hatpin. A hatpin! Goody

Tumtops threatened them with her broom to stop the two of 'em coming to blows."

"McFeck just now told me they were brave."

"No matter their age. Ye said ye saw the ships, Mum. So did I. They weren't chavvie inventions and they look like they spell moil[4] for honest Free Traders. These chavvies are the only ones we know who got up close and personal with these particular Rozzers. I reckoned that mayhap ye'd be wanting to parlay with 'em. See what they can learn us.[5]"

I nodded approvingly. Part of Nellie's decision had been wise, the children might have useful information and there were Rozzers out there machine-gunning peaceable Owlers minding their own business. "We'll have to find out what those Rozzer airships are," I conceded. "Howsumever, the chavvies be strangers. Why bring em here?"

"Zackly what I said," the maid muttered. "Why can't Hastings and Rottingdean look after their own? We got enough trouble as it is taking care of our own poor folk, without all of these furriners from faraway places turning up as strays and scrounging off us."

Nellie looked at her sternly. "Being the pious church-goer ye are, Breksid, I would have expected ye to be familiar with what the Good Book has to say about charity."

---

[4] Trouble: Broad Sussex idiom.
[5] Teach: Broad Sussex idiom usage.

Breksid snorted, then resumed treating the boy's injuries. She did so tenderly enough, her grumpiness a permanent characteristic it seemed.

"The Mairemaid is our base," I pointed out. "There are other safe places, more secluded ones."

"I like 'em." Nellie shrugged. "They're bettermost chavvies…the girl, Liss. There's something about her, something special. We connected like we've known each other forever and longer. Mayhap it won't hurt me to forge friendships along the coast.

"Bettermost to trust naun at all," I said, although I knew Nellie had formed her own opinion on that matter.

"Zackly, jess so," Breksid muttered.

"Asides," my voice took on a lighter note. "Weren't ye busy enow 'forging' friendship with Sam from the Old Bell?"

Nellie blushed.

"Can't trust them Bell-Ends from the Old Bell," Breksid advised. "They got their end of town, we got ours."

I relented. If I wanted Nellie to run the Mairemaid and the Mudlarks someday, that involved allowing her to grow into the role by taking decisions. If I ordered the chavvies to be moved now, all would know I had countermanded Nellie's instructions

Nellie gently rolled the girl onto her back, tutting at the lacerations that criss-crossed the girl's limbs.

I stared at the girl's face, frozen to the spot, forgetting to breathe for a moment.

<u>Scylla</u>
Kill it.

<u>Tess</u>
It couldn't be. There were myriad explanations, perfectly logical, to suggest I might easily be wrong. Yet I knew I wasn't. I knew beyond any doubt who this child was.

"Kill it," Scylla said once again, with a vengeful conviction that told me she wasn't speaking in jest as she sometimes does about these matters.

I shook my head.

"Then take it outside," Scylla advised. "The both of them. Boot them out of the inn. Send them back to the marshes. Let the Sky Gods decide their fate and there won't be blood on your hands."

"I won't," I said softly.

"How often have you secretly dreamed of having such power?" Scylla asked, rhetorically because she and I knew the answer fully well. "Kill it."

"I won't do that," I answered more firmly.

"Mum?" Nellie looked at me with concern in her eyes and voice. "Who are you talking to?"

I stared at her with consternation, before I muttered "nobody" and then fled the Blue Room.

I stopped briefly by the taproom, to establish all was well. The bar staff were coping with the extra business. As I had hoped, the ale, gin, and Brandywine flowed in copious quantities.

The band had just ended a song. Duke Box walked to the front, infectious joy shining on his face. "Ladies and Gents. Marsh Folk and Furriners. Let's welcome to the stage, all the way from the Garish Theatre in Lichfield…"

Three people stepped forward, two men and a woman, all three dressed as gentry. The woman wore a long black skirt, but other than that her attire was masculine, including black coat, black waistcoat, a paisley shirt, old fashioned cravat rather than a bow tie, and top hat. Her dark hair was done up in twin coils that curved along in perfect alignment with the curl of the brim of her hat.

"Here to entertain you," Duke Box continued with an elaborate flourish of his arm. "Johnny Moonstruck, Charles Wainright, and none other than the indomitable Joyce Jameson!"

Like I said before, Sinneport is isolated and we're less likely to know the ins and outs of popular entertainment, but to judge by the enthusiasm with which the announcement was greeted, some of our marsh folk had heard of this lot before.

"Thank you, thank you," Joyce Jameson spoke with a gracious smile. "We'd like to perform 'Burlington Belles."

This was greeted by more cheers as the musicians started a new tune and the theatre folk began to sing.

Oh for the love of it
Oh for the hate of it
Oh for the "Damn, nearly getting away with it"
Oh for the sighing and rueing the day of it
Oh for those Belles.

Confident that the taproom didn't require immediate attention, I strode away through the panelled corridor that led deeper into the inn, the voices of the Lichfield group still audible.

Ain't that always the way of it
Oh My! Oh I was taken in!

I made my way down the stairs, into the cellars, needing some time alone, to think, to contemplate the wages of sin the Lichfield group sang about with such cheerful jollity.

There was a small room behind the central chamber, where Nellie and I kept our Free Trader disguises. Nellie was wearing the Neeva outfit still, but my things…

Scylla

…our things...

Tess

…were there, adorning a mannequin fashioned from interwoven willow reeds.

Unlike the dark cloaks and clothing worn by the Mudlarks, this outfit was magnificent and elaborate. The dress wasn't practical and not worn out on runs,

rather, it was designed to impose and impress. Accompanying it was a wig in the form of sea weeds cascading down, and an elegant masquerade mask in the shape of a skull.

This was the outfit of Scylla, the Mairemaid of Sinneport. Mothers all along the coast, from Chichester to Folkestone, warned their children to be good or else Scylla and her Mudlarks would come to fetch them and drag them kicking and screaming into the marshlands. Free Traders along the coast spoke her name in hushed, reverent tones, emphasising that the Mairemaid of Sinneport was not to be crossed.

Of late, Nellie had worn the disguise too, leaving me free to observe from the side lines dressed as Neeva. It was a useful extra layer of disguise, and a gambit we hadn't shared with anyone else. I suspected that Pug, McFeck, and my other old Parsevals weren't fooled by it, but I knew I could rely on their discretion.

I was aware of subtle differences, of course, in Scylla the Mairemaid's performances. Nellie and I were of a similar build and she had studied my mannerisms well. Voice wasn't an issue, because Scylla's costume had a voice distorter that transformed our voices into a mechanical rasp, meaning the slight differences in our tone and intonation made no difference. It was only disguised as Neeva that we had to mind our voices.

The crucial giveaway, as far as I was concerned, were the words spoken that revealed underlying thoughts. My Free Trader daughter was good at playacting ruthlessness when required, but she lacked the steeled, cold-blooded killer instinct required by my former trade.

I stared at the skull mask. The empty eye sockets stared back.

Scylla

The girl.

Tess

Like a ghost of sorts, truly the dead walk among us this night.

I hadn't wanted my memories to run their full course.

Had I not paid my dues, relived my pains with pounding headaches and helpless rage? Must I relive my mistakes for evermore?

Some six years after my purchase of the Mairemaid, six years of watching Nellie grow into a lively little girl, and six years of working hard to establish the Mudlarks as Free Traders to be reckoned with, I overheard a conversation between Brighton fishermen who had hastily set their hogboats on a course to Sinneport to avoid coarse weather.

From their words I gathered that Hawkeye too had returned to England, no longer a privateer but chief now of the Rottingdean Free Traders and making a name for himself.

My first reaction had been scorn. Too good for a pirate's life, Hawkeye hadn't objected to Free Trading? That had turned into quiet satisfaction that we were both trying our hands at the same profession.

As I gleaned more information about Hawkeye's new career and growing reputation, a tiny seed of hope was planted in my mind, or was it my heart? Regardless, I came to think, I persuaded myself, that we may not have matched as pirate and privateer, but hadn't we both started anew on equal footing as Free Traders?

Scylla objected, fought me tooth and nail, and did what she could to extinguish my hope to lay eyes on Hawkeye again. To no avail, the notion had taken root, grew into longing, and then a driving desire.

Why not? We had been so good together, so right together in all other respects.

I made a momentous decision, which I deemed to be a generous gesture on my part. I decided to forgive Hawkeye. Forgive and forget.

Still, many months passed before I gathered enough courage to journey west. First to Brighton, where I behaved most uncharacteristically by shopping for clothes and having my hair done, wanting Hawkeye to be as astonished as possible when we met again. I did not send word, and doubted he knew I too was in Sussex again, as my own reputation as Free

Trader was based on Scylla's name and Scylla he knew not.

How naïvely excited I had been when I travelled on to Rottingdean. Exhilarated, lost in girlish dreams about our impending reunion, the laughter and delight when he'd sweep me up in his arms, but also thrilled by more base desires.

The gods love irony. The bloody cruel bastards must have had a right laugh at my expense that day, the worst possible day I could have picked to visit the small fishing village.

I saw my Hawkeye again, just as I had fervently wished for. Arm-in-arm with his glowing bride as they departed the church, both their faces delirious with happiness, the church bells ringing joyously.

He saw me not. When his head began to turn my way, an unexpected and uninvited late guest to his wedding, I ducked behind a large row of gravestones, trying to breathe, just about the most complex task I could tackle in that stunned moment.

I returned to Sinneport an empty shell, thunderstruck and devoid of emotions as I dared not let them near. I spent months in grief, torn between the pain of a heart once again ripped asunder, and sheer hatred which I directed at Hawkeye, his bride, but most of all myself. How utterly stupid and foolish I'd been.

It was in those days that Scylla effectively ran the business, coming to the fore like never before, and I let her, grateful to be granted space to nurse my wounds.

I never saw Hawkeye again. He was killed by Rozzers a few years ago. They had ambushed him returning from a run over the Channel. Having convinced myself I hated the man with every fibre of my being, I didn't grieve. However, considering the amount of times I had wished him dead, slowly and painfully so, I felt no satisfaction either, just numbing emptiness that was an echo of my pitiful state after visiting Rottingdean.

I had only seen the brabagious draggle-tail[6] that Hawkeye married just the once, but her face was burned into my memory. In due course I learned her name: Clara Gunn from Brighton, as well as finding out they'd had a daughter.

A daughter who, I now knew, was a spitting image of her mother.

Scylla

Kill it.

Tess

Nellie's voice, her words replayed in my mind. "Like we've known each other forever and longer."

Our daughters have become friends?

Could I let that happen? Risk the one thing I was truly proud of in life, the one person who I loved

---

[6] Neither word is suitable for work, or your tender ears. Broad Sussex idiom.

unconditionally, by exposing yet another Hawkhurst to a Hawkeye?

Perhaps my mind was playing tricks on me. All Hallow's Eve. Old memories and regrets conjured up by tonight's music. The tendency of older age to dwell in the past and amplify nostalgia.

It could be pure coincidence that the girl in the Blue Room was from Rottingdean. More folk lived there than just Hawkeye's draggle-tail and their brat. And wasn't anything other than that simply too coincidental to even be real?

I had to know for sure. Before I did anything rash, foolish…or wise.

I took a last look at Scylla's outfit. Regal, befitting a smuggling queen, a disguise which had become so more than just that.

I went back upstairs, slowly, my body aching from tension. I felt old beyond my years. Force of habit drove me to the taproom first, to hear the close of a song about Lye Street.

Duke Box followed with another elaborate introduction as if he were welcoming royalty. "Come here tonight from Brighton, ladies and gents, misfits and miscreants, please give a hearty welcome to…Mishkin!"

A woman made her way to the fore of the group of musicians. She had compelling eyes, short bright red hair that barely reached her shoulders, and a face that was young still yet seemed haunted by too much knowledge of life's hardships. Her presence was enough to hush the taproom into a silence, laden with anticipation.

The musicians began to play, drums and guitars launching into a tune that caused goose bumps to tickle my arms and legs. It was a sound I'd never expected to hear in the Mairemaid. It was a sound that transported me thousands of miles and many years away: The distinctive rhythm of a tangomão tune.

Mishkin began to sing, her voice one of raw emotive power.

> *The road to ruin is paved*
> *With the backs of the brave*
> *And all the pretty things they said*
> *I myself walked that path*
> *And indeed surpassed*
> *All the stupid limits I set*
> *But if I only knew then what I still don't know now,*
> *Would I plough on ahead, or turn it around?*

I stood rooted to the spot for a moment, torn between my desire to rush upstairs to determine the truth of this mysterious girl…

<u>Scylla</u>

…and kill it…

…and an insane urge to move closer to the musicians and dance with a ghost.

> *Would I pick myself up*
> *From my deep pile rug*
> *And realise one day,*
> *Enough is never enough.*

The lyrics were too close for comfort and I fled the taproom, nearly bumping into Nellie and Sam in the panelled hall. Nellie was back in her regular dress, face hastily wiped clean of face paint. The two young people were entirely oblivious to my presence, locked in a tight embrace, eyes shut, and lips welded together.

I ignored them and rushed on, the distinctive tangomão rhythm and Mishkin's voice seeming to follow me with dogged persistence.

The wages of sin, it's a bottle of gin
And memories you'd rather forget.
It's growing old alone, so bitter, so cold
Add ice, lemon, and regret.

Pug had taken McFeck's place by the door of the Blue Room, seated on a chair, pistol on his lap. The tattered garments were gone. Pug saluted me with his hook but said nothing as I entered the room and closed the door behind me again.

The room was quiet, dimly lit by a candle left burning in its holder on the dresser. The children were asleep, but the girl at least, must have been awake, for her bed was empty. She had climbed into the boy's bed, and the two had snuggled into an innocent embrace, fast asleep.

I picked up the candle and walked to the bed slowly, hesitantly, fearing the girl would wake and not knowing if she'd open her eyes to see my confusion or Scylla's vengeful countenance.

If looks could kill, Scylla would have probably murdered us all at that moment without a moment's thought. She stared at me with icy disdain and contempt, thinking me weak.

She had never forgiven me for wrestling back control after I had emerged from my Rottingdean stupor. She'd done a good job but would have run the Mairemaid and the Mudlarks into the ground in the long run, never able to think like an innkeep or Free Trader, it was the pirate's life for her until the end. I had drawn the line at keelhauling captured Rozzers, it would only have escalated tensions in Romney Marsh.

I sat down on the bedside, searching the girl's face. The resemblance between this Liss and her mother was stronger even than that between Nellie and I, but I could see hints of Hawkeye as well.

So it *was* her. The daughter of my nemesis, who was probably unaware of my existence, but who had stolen Hawkeye's heart from me nonetheless. Hawkeye's little girl. Here in the lion's den, unprotected and in my power.

I reached out a trembling hand, then quickly drew it back when I sensed Scylla tried to take control of my hand, beginning to form a claw.

Clutching my hands together, I sat there, looking at the children.

The Blue Room was located close to the taproom, and I could hear Mishkin continue to sing below.

Older now, but still not the sow
You predicted upon our retreat
Oh, and how many times has my vengeful mind,
Had your head on a plate by my feet.

<u>Scylla</u>

His head on a plate. Don't deny it. You yearned for it. We yearned for it.

And now, now we have something Hawkeye would have considered far more precious than his own head. You know what he was like, this little girl would have been his treasure, the gleaming gold bullion of his eye.

They nearly crushed you, Tess my dear. Would you have pulled through if I hadn't been there? They came so close to breaking you entirely, and now, now it's payback time.

Send her severed head back to Rottingdean so all may know that neither El Escorpion nor Scylla the Mairemaid of Sinneport should ever be crossed.

You dreamt of revenge. It is yours to take. You earned it. Do it. Do it now.

<u>Tess</u>

It was a frozen scene of serenity, yet also a battleground. I had never fought such a dreadful battle as this one before. Scylla alternated between raining down her scorn on me, pleading for vengeance, and demanding the girl be killed.

I persisted in not heeding her torrent of angry words and ferocious emotions.

Waging war against children wasn't the pirate's way, nor the Free Trader's way, nor did I want to make it my own way. I stared hard at the children as I tried to shut Scylla out.

They looked so peaceful, so young still. The way they clung on to each other was endearing, scared no doubt after seeing their crews die in front of their eyes and running through the marsh for their lives; frightened, alone, and far away from home.

My mind jumped from the innocent embrace in

front of my eyes, to the far less innocent business Nellie had been up to with Sam when I swept past them in the corridor, to languid tropical embraces with Hawkeye, and then the raging ruin I'd been left in.

Some of those experiences no doubt awaited these two, their current innocence replaced by instinctive curiosity, and then that headlong rush to experience the joys and delights that always held the danger of turning sour. Ever on it went, these inevitable circles, the turning wheel of fortune, the replays of human nature. The mere thought of it all was exhausting.

But if I only knew then what I still don't know now
What could I do? Change?
No diamond or dream, sovereign or bean
Could buy back even one of those days.

I recalled what the Wise Woman had said in the taproom.

While there are green leaves on the trees, something of summer remains. When the last leaves have gone, winter has come.

My winter was starting, even though I'd been resisting it. Perhaps it was time to accept it and live it in the peaceful serenity I'd once imagined I longed for.

Yes, I could have taken my revenge and shattered the life of Clara Gunn in the same way she had once unwittingly reduced mine to dark nothingness. But in doing so I'd terminate the future of this young girl and be destroying Nellie's reputation, for she had taken this young girl under her protection. Hospitality, once extended, was sacred. Must children suffer for their parents' sins?

Once again, I extended my hand. It wasn't trembling this time as I softly stroked the girl's forehead.

She shifted slightly in response, and without waking mumbled: "Mum?"

I fought back an overwhelming wave of sadness. "No, my dear," I said softly. "But I could have been."

That realisation, that admission, sent Scylla reeling into a retreat, screaming shrilly but ineffectually.

"And I wish I had been," I added.

But if I only knew then, what I still don't know now,
   I'd rather had nothing than live without.
   So here's to us my dear, and here's to the past
   And to think they said, you and I'd never last.

I bent over and kissed the girl's forehead. A tear fell from my eye onto her cheek, and I gently wiped it away.

When I straightened, I felt a hand on my shoulder. Nellie had entered the room with Free Trader's silent tread and joined me.

"Shouldn't ye be driving yer young man wild?" I asked.

"Sam bain't half the man I think he is, if he bain't willing to abide patiently when I'm worried about my mum."

I smiled, raised my hand to my shoulder to lay it upon hers and squeeze it lightly. "Bethanks, but I'm alright now."

I looked around. Scylla was gone. Entirely. It was over. Inside, a bittersweet mix of relief but also regret because I knew I would miss she who had been my constant companion for so many years.

I rose to my feet, the burden of age less painful now. "Come, those damned musicians will be finished soon, we ought to be in the taproom when they do."

Nellie went to the bar when we reached the taproom and brought me a gin.

"With lemon and ice," she said. "Howsumever, I'm afraid we've plain run out of regret."

I laughed. "Don't worry, I have enow for all. This round is on me."

I looked at the ceiling, in the direction of the room where the children slept – safely, under my protection. I'd set out extra guards tonight, just in case Rozzers were still looking for her. I'd help the girl get back home, back to her mother, and Clara Gunn would never know what that cost me, but perhaps Hawkeye, wherever he was, would see…and know.

The logs in the fire shifted, sending sparks rising up into the chimney. I raised my glass to the hearth in silent toast.

Here's to us, my dear, and here's to the past. To think they said you and I would never last.

Ye Sky Gods, but three times lucky I suppose, Hawkeye and Hawkhurst allied again, a new hawkish venture.

The music had come to an end. Grizzly-man, Prospector, and Sailor approached me, expectancy on their faces.

I stared at them balefully for a moment. There was a great deal of understanding in their eyes, suggesting their arrival at the Mairemaid wasn't coincidental. Had they been grinning, their eyes triumphant at the outcome of their shenanigans, I might have been tempted to favour a retaliation of sorts. However, the understanding in their eyes was accompanied only by genuine respect.

Sighing, I admitted, "Ye moved me. Ye'll receive double pay on the morn. Howsumever…"

"There's always a 'but', isn't there?" Sailor asked the others.

"Two, as a matter of fact," I told him. "The first is that ye leave on the morrow and never come back."

"As you wish," Grizzly-man said. "Our work here is done."

"The second?" Prospector asked.

"Play me a few more songs," I said. "Please. I feel like dancing."

"That we can do!" Grizzly-man grinned. "Any preferences?"

"Do you know more tangomão?" I asked hopefully.

"Aye-aye, Cap'n," Sailor brought his knuckles to the rim of his tricorne.

I smiled, then looked at Nellie, stretching out my hand. "Come on, Dear, I've got a few things to learn you yet."

THE END

ABOUT THE AUTHOR

Told once too often that he spends too much time in his imagination, **Nils Nisse Visser** moved there on a permanent basis, having located it in Brighton, Sussex. He's embarked on a rather insane quest to retell old Sussex folklore (and some Dutch sealore) within the genre of historical fantasy, including Smugglepunk (his own take on Steampunk). Entering his fifties, Visser hopes to become a pirate when he grows up.

www.nilsnissevisser.co.uk

CONTRIBUTING AUTHORS

Penny Blake comes from a storytelling background and writes Steampunk and Mythpunk inspired by her Rromani and Celtic heritage.

www.blakeandwight.com

Nimue Brown writes poetry, magazine articles, newsletters, mumming plays, short stories, flash fiction, songs, odd little cartoons about drama llamas, non-fiction books about Paganism, and speculative novels. Some of this is because she has a low boredom threshold, and some of it is because she is far too easily persuaded...

She also writes and colours for the graphic novel series Hopeless Maine, and its various tentacular offshoots. Aside from the short story in this collection, there is also a Hopeless Maine role play game, two illustrated prose novels, assorted music and performance material, and a community site where people who want to play with the island, do so.

The Hopeless Maine blog -
https://hopelessvendetta.wordpress.com

ABOUT THE PHOTOGRAPHER

I have been working with Corin Spinks since 2014. He's Sussex born, so as stubborn as a goat and never does entirely what I ask of him. I kindly forgive him for assuming to know more about of his area of expertise than I do (cause I sometimes take a snap shot with my phone camera, you know, which makes me quite the photographer), simply because the results are always stunningly magnificent.

Corin has done many of my covers, as well as promo-shots, and invaluable help with local homeless projects in Brighton. He also contributes to the stories by sending me images out of the blue, challenging me to write them into stories. About half the characters in *Amster Damned*, as well as some crucial plot elements, resulted from impromptu, unplanned input by Corin.

On this cover, Tess Hawkhurst is kindly modelled by Lara Blair from Shimmy Armageddon & The Boxes of Chaos Performance Troupe.

Over the last five years it's been a pleasure to see a growing appreciation of Corin's work, as well as increasing professional recognition.

Check out his work here:

www.flickr.com/photos/corinography

ABOUT THE STORY

The story **'Wages of Sin'** takes place on an evening that crosses the path of the novel *Fair Night for Foul Folk*, which recounts a smuggling run gone bad from the perspective of Alice Kittyhawk, the young Hawkeye from this story. This includes Alice's short stay at the Mairemaid Inn (Mermaid Inn) of Sinneport (Rye), and encounter with Tess, Scylla, Neeva, and Nellie.

Both 'Wages of Sin' and *Fair Night for Foul Folk* can be read separately from each other but reading both will reveal satisfying overlap.

The visitors from the Garish Theatre in Lichfield, namely Joyce Jameson, Johnny Moonstruck, and Charles Wainright are minor characters from Penny Blake's novel *The Curious Adventures Of Smith and Skarry*.

The introductory words on Samhain/All Hallow's Eve have been gathered from various blogs written by Nimue Brown.

Duke Box is greatly thanked for his input regarding his own character.

In his *Captain Pugwash and the Great Reward*, John Ryan called Rye 'Sinkport', as a wordplay on Cinque Ports, the medieval confederation of south-eastern ports of which Rye was a part.

I've changed Sinkport to Sinneport to also allude to Russell Thorndike's Dr Syn and his Romney

Marsh smugglers, and by happy coincidence or fateweavers' design, it also ties into the title of the song *Wages of Sin* by The Dark Design.

The Mermaid Inn was named the Barmaid Inn by Ryan. 'Mairemaid' is an approximation of how 'mermaid' was pronounced in 19th century Rye. The Mermaid Inn dates back to medieval times. It was visited by William Shakespeare and The Lord Chamberlain's Men, who likely performed *Love's Labour's Lost* there. In later years it was frequented by members of the infamous Hawkhurst Gang, who drank and boasted with their guns and cutlasses openly on the tables.

I am grateful to Judith Blincow of the Mermaid Inn for granting us an opportunity to recreate the Hawkhurst gang scenes in her taproom in the company of assorted misfits.

All images by Yuliya Nazaryan, licensed by Dreamstime.

FEATURED SONGS

Bell Bottom Trousers – A huge 19th century music hall hit.

Smuggler – Traditional Scottish, adapted by author.

Smuggler's Daughter – Traditional, adapted by author.

Blow the Man Down – Shanty, traditional.

Samhain Song – written by Nimue Brown, used with kind permission.

Oh My Love is Gone – Traditional Sussex, minor adaptions by author.

Burlington Belles – Chorus from a music hall song written by Penny Blake for *The Curious Adventures Of Smith And Skarry*, used with kind permission.

Wages of Sin – By The Dark Design, sung by Mishkin Fitzgerald on the *12 Tall Tales* album.

NOTES ON ALICE

Alice Kittyhawk, aka Alice Gunn, aka Liss Hawkeye is the central character of:

Sussex Steampunk Tales / Smugglepunk Tales

Steam Smugglers of Southshire,

The Time Flight Chronicles.

Image of 'Alice Kittyhawk' by photographer Heijo Van De Werf. This image was used for the cover of Rottingdean Rhyme and the same model features on the covers of Them that Ask No Questions and Fair Night for Foul Folk. The model's first name, I was delighted to discover, is Alice.

Alice's story starts with the *Sussex Steampunk Tale* novella *Rottingdean Rhyme*, which was originally written as *The Rottingdean Rhyme* for the Writerpunk Press anthology: *What We've Unlearned, English Class goes Punk*.

It continues with various *Steam Smugglers of Southshire* stories, a collaborative effort with Daren Callow's *Tales of New Albion* podcasts. The first story in this series is entitled: *A Sea Voyage on Wheels*.

The novella *Them that Ask no Questions*, picks up where *Rottingdean Rhyme* left off, and is set in Brighton. It will be followed by the novel *Fair Night for Foul Folk*, set in Rye and Hastings.

Further short stories will follow in various anthologies in 2019/2020 including *Wages of Sin, Jewels From the Deep, The Skirring Dutchman, Sussex by the Sea,* and *Secrets of the Seven Sisters*.

Longer works are planned including the novels: *We Wunt be Druv, Sussex Rising!, For the Love of a Republic,* and *The Rock-a-Nore Murders*.

All the stories can be read as stand-alone stories, or else as part of a series.

The *Time Flight Chronicles*, of which the first book, *Amster Damned,* was published a few years ago, follow Alice as an adult and private investigator who gets embroiled in temporal displacement in search of her childhood friend Dr Braxton Beesworth.

Older Alice. Picture by Jack Savage.
Model Amelia Anna.